Welcome to
The Giggle Club

The Giggle Club is a collection of new picture books made to put a giggle into early reading. There are funny stories about a contrary mouse, a dancing fox, a turtle with a trumpet, a pig with a ball, a hungry monster, a laughing lobster, an elephant who sneezes away the jungle and lots more! Each of these characters is a member of **The Giggle Club**, but anyone can join: just pick up a **Giggle Club** book, read it and get giggling!

Turn to the checklist on the inside back cover and tick off the Giggle Club books you have read.

TEE HEE!

HA HA!

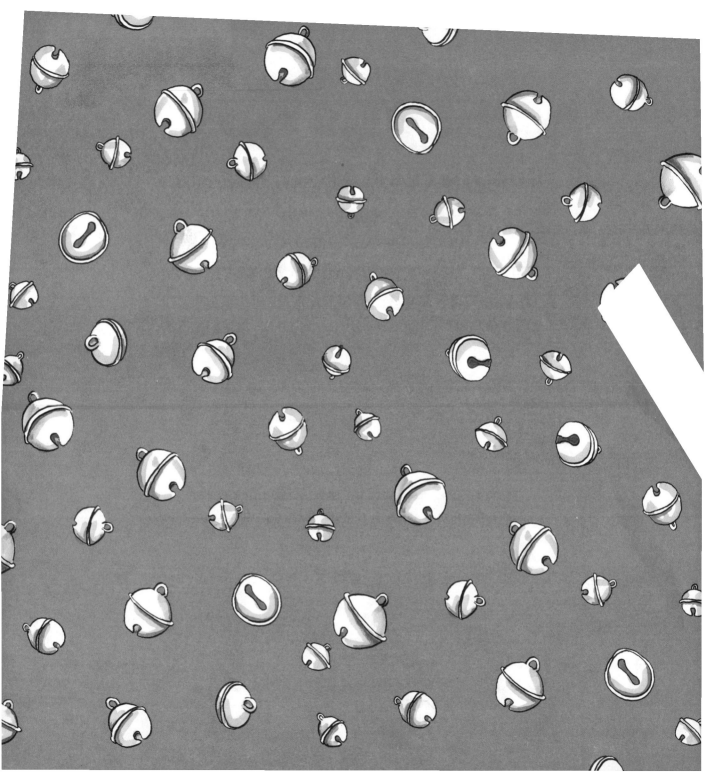

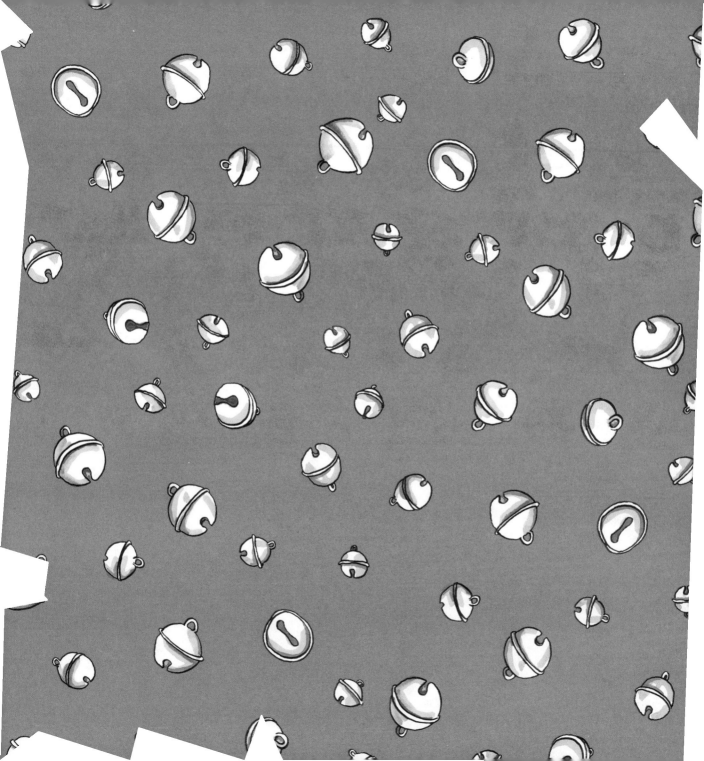

For Fergus

First published 1995 by Walker Books Ltd
87 Vauxhall Walk, London SE11 5HJ

This edition published 1997

10 9 8 7 6 5 4 3

© 1995 Anita Jeram

This book has been typeset in Columbus.

Printed in Hong Kong

British Library Cataloguing in Publication Data
A catalogue record for this book is
available from the British Library.

ISBN 0-7445-4783-0

Anita
Jeram

Daisy Dare

WALKER BOOKS
AND SUBSIDIARIES
LONDON · BOSTON · SYDNEY

Daisy Dare did things her friends were far too scared to do.

"Just dare me," she said.
"Anything you like.
I'm never, *ever* scared!"

So they dared her to walk
the garden wall.

They dared her to eat a worm.

They dared her to stick
out her tongue
at Miss Crumb.
And she did!

One day,
Daisy's friends
thought of a really
scary dare to do.

They whispered it to Daisy.

"I'm not doing that!" she said.

"Daisy Dare-not!" they laughed.

Daisy took a deep breath. "All right," she said. "I'll do it." This was the dare: to take the bell off the cat's collar.

The cat was asleep. That was good.

The bell slipped off easily. That was good too.

But Daisy's hands
trembled so much
that the bell
tinkled, the cat woke up ...

and that was
very,
very
bad!

Daisy ran and ran
as fast as she could,
back to her friends,
through the
garden
gate, and into the house
where the cat
couldn't follow.

"Phew!" said Billy.
"Wow!" gasped Joe.
"You're the bravest,
most daring mouse in the whole
world!" shouted Contrary Mary.
Daisy Dare grinned with pride.
"Just dare me," she said.
"Anything you like…

I'm only *sometimes* scared!"

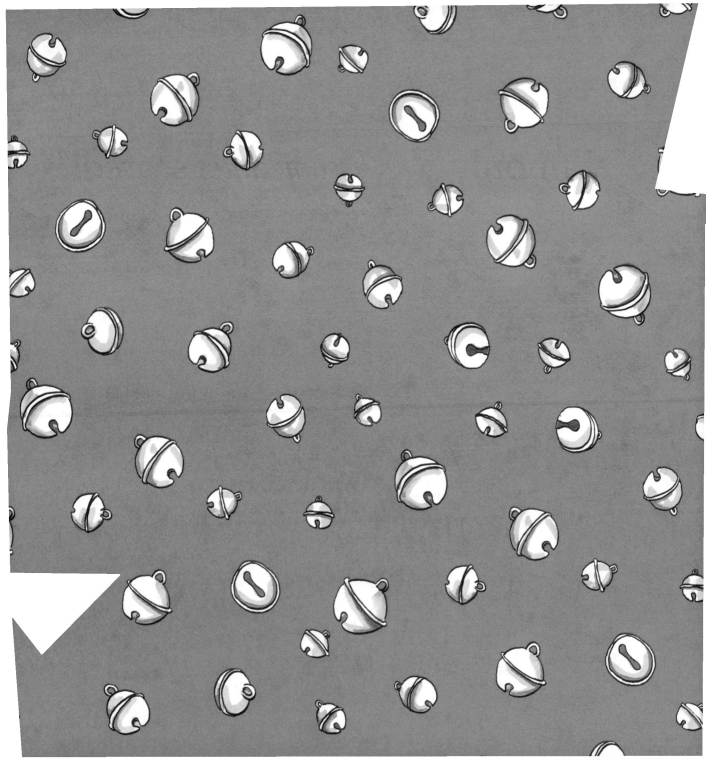

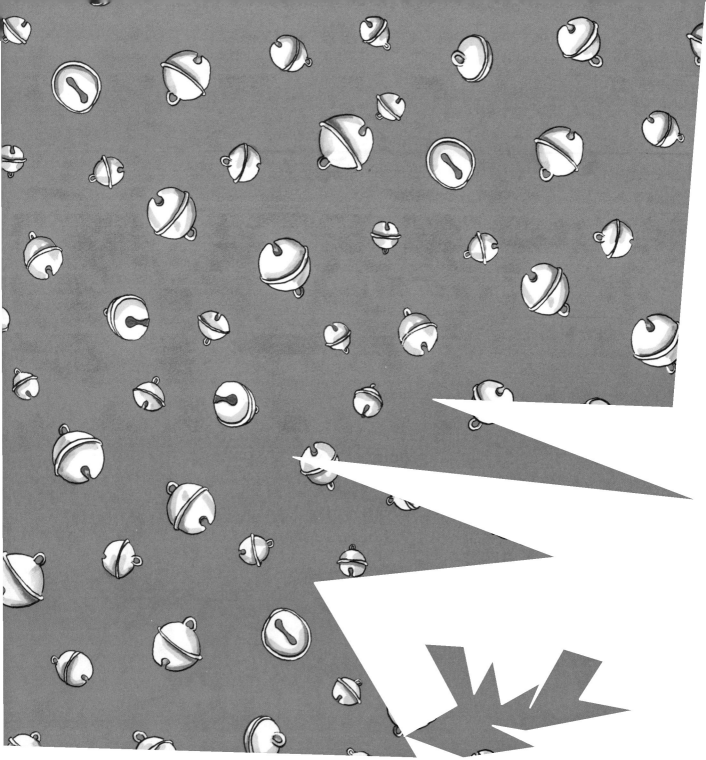